THE LAST 5 YEARS

Music and Lyrics by
Jason Robert Brown

The original Off-Broadway cast recording of *The Last Five Years* was released by
Sh-K-Boom Records, 4001-2.

For information on performance rights for *The Last Five Years* contact:

Music Theatre International
421 W. 54th Street
New York, NY 10019
phone: 212-541-4684
fax: 212-397-4684
website: www.mtishows.com

ISBN 0-634-04828-7

HAL•LEONARD®
CORPORATION
7777 W. BLUEMOUND RD. P.O. BOX 13819 MILWAUKEE, WI 53213

In Australia Contact:
Hal Leonard Australia Pty. Ltd.
22 Taunton Drive P.O. Box 5130
Cheltenham East, 3192 Victoria, Australia
Email: ausadmin@halleonard.com

Visit Hal Leonard online at
www.halleonard.com

THE LAST FIVE YEARS opened Off-Broadway on March 3, 2002, at the Minetta Lane Theatre in New York, with René Scott as Cathy, Norbert Leo Butz as Jamie, directed by Daisy Prince. The show was originally produced in 2001 at Northlight Theatre Company, Skokie, Illinois.

The Last Five Years is a show about a relationship, about a marriage. It's told from two angles. From the man's point of view, it starts at the first meeting and ends in the present, when the marriage breaks up. From the woman's point of view, it starts in the present and works back in time to the first meeting. Only at the wedding, in the center of the one-act evening, do the stories intersect. The audience has to do some thinking to track the two stories, but the clues are all there.

–Richard Maltby, Jr.
excerpted from the CD liner notes

Music and Lyrics by Jason Robert Brown

Show Vocal Selections:

00313206	The Last Five Years
00313148	Parade
00313188	Songs for a New World

CONTENTS
in show order

STILL HURTING

Music and Lyrics by
JASON ROBERT BROWN

Give me a day,___ Ja - mie! Bring back the lies,___ Hang them

back on the wall!_____ May - be I'd see How you could be_____ So cer - tain that

Once the foun - da - tion's cracked And

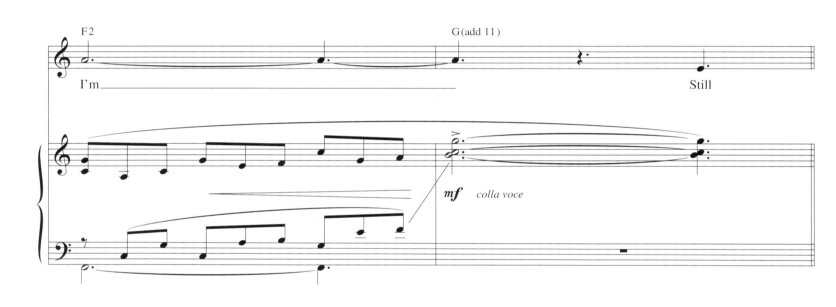

I'm _____ Still

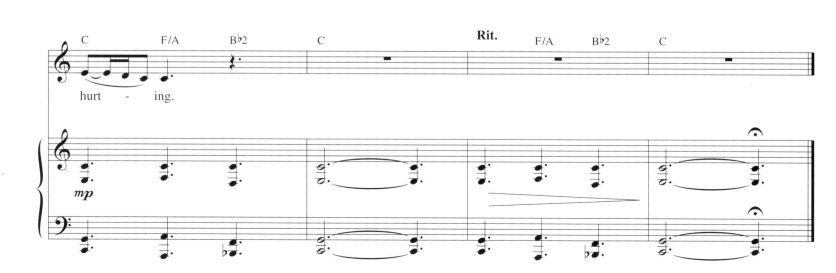

hurt - ing.

SHIKSA GODDESS

Music and Lyrics by
JASON ROBERT BROWN

MOVING TOO FAST

Music and Lyrics by
JASON ROBERT BROWN

Funky Rock 4 (♩ = 100-102)

Did I just hear an a - larm____ start____ ring - ing?

Did I see si - rens go fly - ing past? Though I don't know what to - mor-

row's bring - ing, I've got a sing - u - lar im - pres - sion things are mov - ing too fast.

I'm glid - ing smooth as a fig - ure____ skat - er, I'm rid - ing hot as a roc-

I'm do - in' things I nev - er dreamed of be - fore!____

We start to take the next step to - geth - er,

Found an a - part - ment on Se - ven - ty - Third!____

The *At - lan - tic Month - ly*'s print - ing my first chap - ter–

A PART OF THAT

Music and Lyrics by
JASON ROBERT BROWN

One day___ we're___ just___ like "Leave It___ to Bea - ver."

One day___ it's___ just___ a Ty - pi - cal___ life,___

THE SCHMUEL SONG

Music and Lyrics by
JASON ROBERT BROWN

Schmu-el would work 'til half-past ten at his tail-or shop in Klim-o-vich,

Get up at dawn and start a-gain__ with the hems and pins and twist.

For-ty-one years had come and gone__ at his tail-or shop in Klim-o-vich.

A SUMMER IN OHIO

Music and Lyrics by
JASON ROBERT BROWN

THE NEXT TEN MINUTES

Music and Lyrics by
JASON ROBERT BROWN

WHEN YOU COME HOME TO ME

Music and Lyrics by
JASON ROBERT BROWN

When you come home to me, I'll wear a sweet-er smile, And hope that, for a while, You'll stay. When you come home to me, Your hand will touch my face And ban-ish an-y trace of gray.

IF I DIDN'T BELIEVE IN YOU

Music and Lyrics by
JASON ROBERT BROWN

I CAN DO BETTER THAN THAT

Music and Lyrics by
JASON ROBERT BROWN

My best friend had a lit-tle sit-u-a-tion at the end of her sen-ior year,

And like a shot, she and Mitch-ell got mar-ried that sum-mer.

NOBODY NEEDS TO KNOW

Music and Lyrics by
JASON ROBERT BROWN

GOODBYE UNTIL TOMORROW

Music and Lyrics by
JASON ROBERT BROWN